Silver Bangles
and
Gold Bangles

with three other short stories

-Be My Daughter

-The Deeds

-Navigating though Loneliness and Aloneness

Nara Somaratne

Publisher: Inspiring Publishers,
P.O. Box 159, Calwell, ACT Australia 2905
Email: publishaspg@gmail.com
http://www.inspiringpublishers.com

 A catalogue record for this book is available from the National Library of Australia

National Library of Australia The Prepublication Data Service

Author: Nara Somaratne
Title: Silver Bangles and Gold Bangles
Genre: Fiction

Paperback ISBN: 978-1-923087-27-9
ePub2 ISBN: 978-1-923087-18-7

Meaning of Sinhala words in this book

Achchi, Appachchi: Father

Amma: Mother

Aiya: Elder brother

Akka: Elder sister

Bappa: Father's younger brother

Chena: Shifting agricultural practice by clearing of forest land

Duwa: Daughter

Kachcheri: Government's District Administrative Office

Loku Amma: Mother's elder sister

Loku Appachchi: Father's elder brother

Lokuputha: Elder son

Loku Mahaththaya: Head master of the school

Mama, Mamandi: Mother's brother, or uncle

Malli: Younger brother

Miniha: Impolite way to call a man or husband

Mudalali: Businessman

Nandamma: Father's sister

Nangi: Younger sister

Punchi Amma: Mother's younger sister, or wife of *Bappa*

Roti: Flat bread

Saree: Principal outer garment of women in Indian subcontinent

Sarong: Large tube or length of fabric wrap around the waist

Veddah: Sri Lankan aboriginal who used to live in the forest

Wedamahaththaya: Village Ayurvedic physician

Silver Bangles and Gold Bangles

A short story

Nara Somaratne

There I was, alone, sitting on the bench outside my unit in the retirement village. The village was quiet, though some residents passed by my unit with their rollators and said hello. In front of my unit, there are two rows of eight units occupied each by single residents, except for Nolan and Jina, who have been husband and wife for over 50 years. They have lived in the village for the last 15 years. Most of the residents are in their mid-80s to early 90s. Nolan is a great volunteer who keeps the village garden neat, not even leaving behind a fallen leaf; he trims the rose bushes and takes the garbage bins out to the road on garbage collection day and brings them back to the village afterwards. He is a big help to the paid maintenance workers and the village manager. Nolan passed by my unit with his sweeper as I sat there and said, 'Hello Senevi,' then added his usual greeting, 'How you are going today, mate?'

The second unit in the row is home to Helen. Residents say she married her husband in the village community hall, but he had fallen sick and been moved into a high care centre elsewhere.

Helen came out and went to her car, greeting me on the way. Twice a day, every day, she goes to see her husband.

A couple of pigeons were still in the front yard, even though it was close to 10 am. Normally they arrive early in the morning and close to sunset. In the village, under the palm trees, there are ants and other insects, so the birds are in abundance. It is generally around this time that residents start to come out of their units and move around, some with just a walking stick and others with their walkers or rollators. Few of the residents move around by themselves.

Most residents go to the community hall for reading; some of the ladies get together to play bingo or get books from the small library. It's beautiful to see, despite their old age, these ladies dressing nicely, and doing their hair and makeup before coming out of their units. Apart from me, very few single men live in the village. Unlike ladies, they usually don't meet for a chat. I had a good friend, Berney who lived on the eastern side of the village with his wife Jane. They originally come from South Africa. Berney and I would meet at one of our units to share a cup of tea and talk about world problems – the impact of climate change, carbon emissions to the atmosphere, civil wars and even food poisoning. It seemed nothing else was important to us; they were minor problems such as paying bills, the next meal, our mobility or health care. It was always world problems – the habitual talk of old people. Berney was a food scientist by profession. He passed away a year ago, and I really miss him.

One regular resident, Penza, passes my unit almost every day by this time. She is the 'noisy girl', who usually goes to see her elder sister Greta who lives in an independent unit outside the main compound of the village. Penza goes there for a chat and for lunch with her sister, who is a good cook.

That particular day as I sat outside was a Sunday, so visitors were starting to arrive – daughters, grandchildren and even pets to show to their grandparents who lived in the village.

I had had my visitors the night before. It was a Saturday evening and my elder son Tirath, his wife Moly and their two daughters, Lily and Carla, came for dinner. As any other grandfather does, I love to see my 'girls', Lily and Carla. My younger son Sirimath, who lives and works in Melbourne was in Adelaide for a holiday and he also joined us for dinner. My daughter, Kumudu, for some unknown reason never comes to the village to see me; instead, we meet once a month to have a coffee or lunch at a restaurant, even though she lives not too far from the village with her mother. Lily and Carla did some paintings in their colouring books while we talked. Moly always had some reading materials and painting books with her so that whenever the children came, they wouldn't get bored. Other times, Lily and Carla took out the family photo albums to look at their daddy's childhood photos with aunty Kumi and uncle Siri. The children call Kumudu 'Kumi' and Sirimath 'Siri'.

Ever since I moved into the village, Moly used to visit with the girls, either for dinner or just a cup of tea, to say hello. This was a good habit to keep the girls' memories refreshed with their paternal grandfather. The little ones called me *Aththa* (grandfather). In February 2020, Moly and the girls brought me a little birthday cake and a candle and had a mini birthday party for me. It was unforgettable – the best I have ever had. How thoughtful that was.

Last evening's visit was a typical one from Tirath and his family. We usually sat down and had a little chat before ordering food. The nearby DeCorso's Pizzeria is famous for Italian food. We ordered pasta for girls and pizza for us. We all enjoyed our meals before the night turned into the ugliest family dinner ever.

Before the family left, the girls came to give me a hug. This was usual and I said, 'Instead of buying other gifts, I will start collecting jewellery for the girls.'

Tirath became angry at this and said, 'Do not by jewellery for the girls. The jewellery you bought for Moly – she doesn't like it. She doesn't even wear it.' He raised his finger and came towards me shouting, 'You bought them for your own pleasure not for anything else! If you want, you can save money for the girls' education, like Moly's parents are doing.'

I thought he was going to hit me.

Moly shouted at him. 'Tirath, Tirath, stop it,' which he did.

The girls and Sirimath were astonished but didn't utter a word. I calmly tried to explain to Tirath that it is a tradition in Sri Lanka and India for parents and grandparents to buy jewellery to give their daughters and granddaughters. I had had the opportunity to buy jewellery for the future wives of my seven- and twelve-year-old sons when I lived in Oman because I had a good salary there, and there was good jewellery available. But there were no ears for my words. I did not know why he asked me to give money to the girls' education. Both Tirath and Moly were medical professionals with a good income. I did not have any savings even though

I was over 70 years of age; I had only just started to save for my pension. All my earnings had been spent on the welfare of my family to give them the best of everything – comfortable middle-class living, overseas travels, a good education and even paying university fees to send them into society loan-free. I never thought about me at any time.

After Tirath's family left, Sirimath stayed with me for few more minutes; unable to talk, we stayed silent but still seemed to be communicating all the same. I said in a low voice that the jewellery was not just gold; it was made of my 'sweat', and not just mine, but that of my poor mother and three elder sisters as well, who had made lots of sacrifices to educate me.

Sirimath said in low voice, 'Yes *Achchi* (father), it is.'

Shortly afterwards, Sirimath also left. I sat on the single seater of the lounge suite. I remembered my mother's only jewellery at the time – a pair of silver bangles.

The emotion was so high, a torrent of tears started to flow.

It was 1962, only nine years after the settlers arrived in Huruluwewa colonisation scheme in northcentral province of Sri Lanka. Since 1960, the area had experienced drought. The water level in the Huruluwewa tank was at its lowest, and many people said the tank bed had been exposed in several places. Some people made a living by catching fish from the tank's shallow waters. Others took their cattle to graze on the weeds and grasses that covered the exposed tank bed. The village we lived in was along the right bank of the main canal in Huruluwewa. As there had been no rain over the last two years, only pockets of water pools could be found along the canal. The water was a muddy, brown colour as the villagers caught fish using nets and wooden traps (*karaka*) in the murky waters. Added to this, water buffalo would come for water and lie down to escape the scorching sun. Dried water lilies and floating and submerged pond weeds covered the canal bed. In places where people could access the canal, they had dug wells for bathing.

Home gardens didn't escape the drought either and most of the shallow wells in the village had also dried up. For water supply in homes, people had to go to those nearby who had deep wells. Whenever our water well dried, we would go next door to Siriya's well. In the morning, before other people came, we would go there with two or three clay pots to bring water home for drinking and cooking. There were no vegetable plots in the garden. Even though land allotment was one and half acres, only a few perennial trees – coconut, cashew nut, lemon – managed to survive. Without water, only the top two or three leaves of banana trees – mostly having dry leaves – remained green. Some of the trees were completely dead and collapsed in the middle.

As there was no green grass for cattle and buffalo, boys took their herds to dried paddy fields for grazing on remaining patches of grasses. Green grass remained along the natural drainage channel networks in the fields. I would go to the paddy fields after school or some weekends with my friends, Karu and Ari. Before the drought, there were beautiful ponds full of water lilies and reeds that were now dried out. There were no water birds any more – heron, egret, cormorant – but occasional nests of weavers could be found on reeds and *attikka* (cluster fig trees) and *kumbuk* (arjun trees). Kumbuk trees are beautiful, standing tall and providing shade from the tropical heat and growing close to water ways.

When my friends and I walked behind grazing buffalo, we had lots to talk about and observe, as we would walk at a slow pace. It was sad seeing the dead carcasses of buffalo rotting in the fields, some with only dried skin and bones remaining. At other locations, bones were scattered all around because stray dogs and foxes would feed on the carcasses. As we approached, dogs would run away and look at their feed eagerly from a distance. The smell was unbearable, and maggots filled the cavities opened by the dogs. Later, we learned that foot and mouth disease had spread in the area, and most of the cattle and buffalo had died.

For bathing, we would walk to a nearby well dug in the drainage canals by villagers or several kilometres to a small village tank where some water was available. We would go there in groups for bathing and washing clothes. Soap was all purpose for us; we never knew there were different soaps for washing clothes and cleaning the body until we grew up.

Without rice farming or *chena* cultivation (shifting agricultural practice by clearing and burning forests), life was extremely difficult for the villagers during drought. Each family received coupons for two measures of rice (about four pounds) for each family member from the cooperative shops once a week. A measure of rice cost 25 cents. As rice was the staple food for all three meals, this amount was insufficient. In addition, each family was given labour work as a government drought-relief measure. Typical work involved repairing earthen irrigation channels, filling potholes on access roads, and clearing and filling breached waterways. This was essential work for water distribution to paddy fields when water was available for irrigation. Most often, people had to walk over a mile to reach their daily workplace. Usually, the adult males and boys would go to work; women were rarely seen.

At our home there was no adult male. Our father died in 1961, and even though I had seven siblings, there was no adult male. My eldest sister did not come to Huruluwewa with us; she stayed with father's younger brother in his house in our ancestral village, Kannehepola, about 7 kilometres from the Kurunegala town. The second (Sudu *Akka*) and fourth sisters (Punchi *Akka*) were in Kurunegala working as domestic servants. The third elder sister (Podi *Akka*) had married and gone to Kokawewa village, at the tail end of the right bank canal with her husband. The only other male (Navé *Aiya*) was just 13, two years older than me and our two younger sisters Seela and Kumari, who were just nine and seven years old.

Sometimes my brother and I would go out with mother to help her with her work. We had two small mamoties (hand tools) to use. The ground was clay and gravel and very hard due to the continued drought; when we hit the ground with our mamoties, they bounced back. Only strong men could do this kind of work, not women or children. What else could we do? Our mother kept working, sweating all over, and her jacket was almost wet through. As I watched her, my eyes filled with tears. For lunch, I would go home and bring *roti* (flat bread) back. Almost all people had roti for lunch, made either from wheat flour or millet flour.

When I was at school, mother carried her lunch and water with her. On those days, she couldn't complete her portion of the work, but young people in the neighbourhood came forward and helped her, saying, 'We will do it for you, Nenda.' It was typical in rural settings in Sri Lanka to use the terms *Mama* (uncle) for men and *Nenda* (aunty) for women, even though they were not related – even with complete strangers. This was a typical way of respecting adults. Usually, the men finished earlier and went home.

Payment was made by distributing wheat flour so that every household at least had roti. Rice was eaten only for dinner. Without this relief, many people would have died from hunger. At the village boutique shops, people talked about wheat flour distribution by the government. Some said those were kind donations received from America and other rich countries. Some other talk was that rich countries had so much food, they also fed their animals and still had an excess amount to give away to poor countries. Whatever the truth of the stories that went around, it was a big help for the villagers.

Eating roti had its funny side too. The village youths played games such as a primitive form of soft ball or cricket known as *Elle*. Elle was a popular bat-and-ball game in Sri Lanka, and also a localised name for slow-pitch softball, often played in rural villages. The wheat flour was so prevalent, boys divided into two teams: the Roti team and the Manioc team. All players wore a *sarong* usually folded up to knee high. Almost everyone was barefoot with no shirt, and typically not wearing underwear either. A witty, talkative boy would be selected for commentary, who would make hilarious comments. The art of cricket commentary was learnt from radio commentators. Radios were rare and usually only available in the boutique shops and in a few houses. All the people who played and came to watch the games had an enjoyable time.

People's living conditions were harsh, although the government's low-cost rice and wheat flour for work scheme gave some relief, but there was no cash for other essential household items, such as sugar, salt, coconut, coconut oil, kerosene for lamps or soap. There was no paid work in the area. Some villagers went away to find labour and would come home at least once a month with their savings. But there was no adult male to do this in our home. Sometimes Sudu *Akka* would send a money order for ten rupees, which was half her monthly salary.

It was common to find mother sitting down and pondering what to do. All she had to pawn to borrow money was her two silver bangles – thick round bangles with a rounded head at each end. This was her only valuable possession.

She wore them proudly.

One time, after sitting and pondering on a bench for a while, she went into the house and came out without her bangles on. They were wrapped in a little white cloth in her hand.

'I am going to Ukkubanda's house to borrow some money and he can keep the bangles as surety,' said mother. A little later she arrived back home with a look of despair on her face. 'They don't have any money either,' she said.

Even though we had rich relatives in our ancestral village, no one cared about our welfare – or even our very existence.

It seemed mother was starting to realise there was *only us for us*.

A little later she said, 'I am going to Badderala's house to see whether I can borrow money.' Again, she took her bangles and went away. As a habit we used to tell other where we were going if we stepped out of the house. We probably learnt this from our mother. This time she managed to get two rupees with the promise that she would pay back three rupees within one month to get her bangles. Every time Sudu *Akka* came forward to rescue her bangles. There was no other way. Once she brought back her bangles, she wore them until the next time she took them somewhere else to borrow money. I do not know how many times it happened; all I knew was mother was not wearing her bangles several times a year.

As there was no money to spend, during the drought, common vegetables cooked at most houses were eggplant, *thibbatu* (cherry eggplant), *elabatu* (Thai eggplant) and small bitter gourd which grew well and could be picked from abandoned chenas in the area. There were a variety of green leaves and root vegetables; leaves of manioc trees; *kathurumurunga* or agati leaves (*Sesbania grandiflora*); *murunga* (moringa); and *anguna kola* (*Tylophora pauciflora*). Usually my younger sisters, Seela and Kumari accompanied mother to go to the chenas to pick vegetables or firewood. Whenever village hunters had game meat, usually venison or wild boar, mother gave us 50 cents to go there and buy a pound of meat, or sometimes she would buy a couple of tilapia fish and cook for us. These were our childhood delicacies.

One of the big consolations for mother was that we did our school studies well, and never went out with the naughty boys in the area who got involved in minor robberies, smoking tobacco or fighting. I was very keen on my studies and determined from a young age to get out of this misery and go back to our ancestral village in Kurunegala. As there was only one chair at home, after school I went back to school to complete my homework and do further reading. Father had paid for a full suite of furniture that our neighhour, carpenter George Botheju, was to make. But since father had died, he never completed it, other than a bed, a chair and an unfinished table.

Usually, the headmaster's sons, Nimal and Wimal, joined me doing their homework on week ends or after school. One day when Podi *Akka* was at home, we were sitting on mats and talking, and *Akka* said, 'Everyone in the village says you are doing your school work well – at least try to get a teaching job.' Then *Amma* (mother) said, 'Try at least to get a clerical job in the village cooperative shop.' Those were their dreams. They were very much desperate that I should get a job somewhere to help relieve the burden of poverty. That was all they could think of at that time.

In October1962, the area received a fair amount of rain at the start of the north-east monsoon season and there was some relief for the farmers. The level of water in the tank was still insufficient for the main cultivation season, starting from September (*Maha season*), but later, in January and Februay, rains were sufficient to issue water for *Yala* season, starting in May.

The works at paddy fields and home gardens restarted. People were busy and life began returning to normal. Whenever someone had been to town, they were always asked, 'How many feet of water did the Huruluwewa Tank receive?' Everyone who passed that way read the water-depth marker written on the concrete slab of the sluice gate. People were that desperate.

After the harvest, in 1964, mother went to Kurunegala and brought Punchi *Akka* home. After the arrival of Punchi *Akka*, the economic situation at home changed completely. She was a very active young lady, and with her savings, she started raising chicken and selling eggs, and growing manioc, vegetables and tobacco which she also sold. She kept all of us very busy. Mother never had to borrow money again or give up her bangles for surety.

The silver bangles were always in her hands.

My studies continued unabated. In year 8 at school, I managed to win a government scholarship for science education and enter the Central College in Kekirawa, a regional town. The high school had many facilities I had never seen before, such as science laboratories, sporting facilities and a hostel where scholars lived. After passing through the G.C.E (OL) examination, I entered Science College in Matale, a reputable high school for science education. From there, after passing the G.C.E (AL) examination, I entered the engineering faculty of the University of Sri Lanka to follow the civil engineering degree course, which I completed in 1978.

Life was not easy along the road. Many difficulties were encountered and faced successfully. Lots of sacrifices were made by mother and my siblings. It was now time to fulfill my family responsibilities. First and foremost, my younger sister Seela's wedding was taken care of. Some friends and I invested our earnings and we had a good return from them.

I was unable to find suitable land or a house to buy in our ancestral village in Kannehapola, so I bought a house in

Mallawapitiya off Kurunegala-Kandy Road. It became the family house for the next two decades.

Meanwhile, a suitable bride for my brother was proposed from neighbouring Nikawewa. The family originally came from Kandy district. After my brother's wedding, my mother and elder sister Punchi *Akka* came to settle down in the Mallawapitiya house with our niece Arty, who grew up in our house from early childhood. I went there on weekends to look after the needs of my family.

By this time, wedding arrangements were taking place for my elder sister Punchi *Akka*. Even though her marriage had been delayed, everyone was happy she had finally found a good person to share her life with. Among other family responsibilities, I started to save money to buy gold jewellery for my sisters. As I wasn't familiar with buying jewellery, I gave money to Punchi *Akka* and asked her to buy jewellery for herself, our two younger sisters and, more importantly, our mother. My mother had never had any gold jewellery in her life. Usually this was a parent's responsibility. But Punchi Akka helped me buy her a necklace, earrings and two gold bangles.

She removed her silver bangles, and tears started to flow down her cheeks as she donned the gold bangles for us all to see.

Time passed quickly. I married a girl proposed by friends, Suramya, in November 1983. She hailed from Udahagama village along the Kandy–Colombo Road, near Peradeniya. In 1984, our son Tirath was born and in 1986, we immigrated to Australia thinking we would work for two years to save money and return to Sri Lanka. Unable to find a suitable job, I continued to study further towards master's and doctoral degrees. This proved to be a successful move, as I then found good employment opportunities.

From my job in Sydney, I moved to the Sultanate of Oman to take up a position in the Ministry of Water Resources. There were lots of jewellery shops in Ruwi. Most of the designs were to attract the expatriate community: Sri Lankans, Indians, Pakistanis and Bangladeshis. It was a traditional custom to provide jewellery for your wife and daughters, as well as gifts for close relatives. We started to collect jewellery for Suramya and my daughter Kumudu, and then expanded to nieces on both sides of the family. After several years, we collected more jewellery for Kumudu than any other girl on both sides of the family had ever had, over generations. One day, a thought came across my mind that, while we only had one daughter at that time, in future there would be two other daughters who would join the family when Tirath and our younger son Sirimath got married, so I started to collect jewellery for our future daughters-in-laws. Tirath was twelve years old and Sirimath was just seven at that time.

It was the jewellery I had bought in Oman at that time for my future daughter-in-law – Moly –that had caused the painful interaction with Tirath the night before.

Buying gold jewellery had brought tears of joy to mother's eyes; buying gold jewellery for my daughter-in-law had brought tears of sadness to my eyes.

The abusive words used by Tirath was not the Sri Lankan way, nor even the Australian way. Instead of words of thanks, he had used abusive language to hurt a hard-working father, not recognising how much of a sacrifice I had made to give him the best chance in life. This once exemplary, brilliant young man had turned into an arrogant irrational person.

Jewellery designs may change over time and locations, as do individual tastes. But the substance never changes – *gold is gold.* People change though. This incident revealed a dark side of human behaviour.

Much later in life we came to know that the silver bangles my mother wore were given to her by her mother in 1930. My mother was just a ten-year-old girl at that time, and a malaria epidemic was widespread in the area. When her mother became ill, being the youngest in the family and the youngest daughter, my mother was always near her bedside, sitting next to her on the floor. Unable to rise from the bed, grandmother had pulled her silver bangles from her hands and put them into my mother's saying, 'Keep them with you all the time; it will be like I am near you, my little girl.' The following day, she died.

These two silver bangles helped to buy us food, sometimes medicine, and even exercise books for school, which allowed me to continue my education.

Perhaps due to the commanding role fathers play as the head of the family, and in some cases, taking disciplinary actions to correct them, some children may find it hard to express the deep love and affection they have for their fathers. Some may even opt to take revenge at a later date, forgetting all the sacrifices he made. No doubt that a mother's love is unparalleled, but this does not mean a father's love is insignificant. A father toils his entire life to ensure his children get the best of everything, to take good care of and protect them from all kinds of dangers and challenges in the outside world. But somehow, a father's love and 'sweat' becomes minor beside that of mothers. Fathers too need to be loved, respected, and honoured for all that they have done to love and nurture their children.

In some rare cases, mothers do and say bad things about fathers to get the total attention and love of their children. How many times had Tirath stopped to think about the sacrifices I, along with my mother and siblings, have made to educate me; eventually benefitting my own family, wife and children. After all, Tirath was now a father too, of two girls. My mother's silver bangles are part of me and a small part of Tirath as well. The history should not be erased.

No matter what happens, whatever they say and do, I love my children as the day they were born. My love for children is best expressed by veteran Sri Lankan singer TM Jayaratne in his song 'Amma Sandaki' (mother is the moon)-written by his wife Malani Jayaratne. The song goes on to say; *while the mother is the Moon, father is the silver Sun in the world; and fathers are totally dedicated to their children, Fathers virtually take a back seat when it comes to singing the praises of parental love; In comparison to the countless number of tributes paid to honour mothers in prose, verse, and art, those done in recognition of fathers are very little; He ponders as to why his blood too did not turn into milk at the strength of that love'.*

* * *

'Hey, Senevi you still sitting there. What are you doing?' It was Penza coming into the village from the back gate. 'I went to get a haircut with Greta at our cousin's saloon. I was looking old, hahaha,' she laughed, and pushed her rollator off towards her unit.

I realised it was around 1 pm, so I went inside to listen to the song 'Amma Sandaki' one more time.

Be My Daughter

A short story

Nara Somaratne

It was the last Sunday in August, a sunny morning but slightly cold, the last of the winter months in Adelaide. My daughter, Kumudu had sent me a text message, and I was waiting at the Taylorblend Café on Hallett Road to have morning coffee with her. I normally go to a place at least 10 minutes early to get a table, and luckily, that day there was an empty table facing the road and playground. The café is at a higher elevation, and you need to climb few steps up from the road level. At 11.30 am in the morning, I saw a white car parked on the roadside and Kumudu stepped out and came towards the café. As she approached the table, I got up went towards her to give her a hug, but she shrugged off my hand and sat down opposite me.

She was bursting with anger and said loudly, 'You apologise to me now, for writing this text message to me.'

'Don't shout,' I said calmly. 'There are other people here – and tell me why?'

'You did not want to see me when your sister was here,' she said bitterly. 'Your sister was much more important than me. And you can listen to Tirath, but not me.'

Tirath is my eldest son, and my younger sister Kumari had recently been staying with me at my unit in the retirement village, on a visit from Sri Lanka.

'I am sorry for that,' I said, to calm her down and keep the daughter-father relationship intact.

'That is not enough,' she replied loudly, 'and you should apologise properly. I'll give you one or two months and see what happens.'

'Don't shout,' I said again, as I could see it was upsetting other customers who were trying to enjoy their meals, snacks and coffee. 'I have gone through many difficulties in life, particularly at the hand of your mother,' I explained. 'I tolerated it all to give my children a better life.' I asked her to read the book I had written, *A Silent Pain*, and told her it would explain all the things that she didn't know about her mother and I.

Her answer was simple. 'We haven't had anything to do with your sister for the last 20 years; we don't care about anyone we haven't seen in over 20 years.'

Her words were flooding out fiercely, just like water released from a flood gate gushing along the river.

'More than that,' she continued, 'we are Australian, not Sri Lankan anymore.' Then she added, as a reminder to me, 'You are also Australian.'

'I am still a villager, in my mind,' I said.

'If she comes to stay with you again, and if I ask you to come for a lunch or coffee, will you come without her?'

My answer was simple: 'Never. I will not hurt her again.'

I realised this was an ultimatum my daughter was giving me – the father who adored her, had given her all the best in life and even called her 'my mother' – a Sri Lankan term of endearment. That was the extent of my love for my only daughter.

Kumudu pushed her chair back and left in a huff.

She knew I had on-going medical conditions and had even had a heart operation. And she also knew perfectly that I don't have anyone here except my children, which is why my sister came to stay. But now …?

This was not the daughter I had known since the day she was born. The last few years since her mother and I had separated had changed her gradually from an innocent girl to a violent woman, at least towards me. That was the impact of living with negative people. No doubt she was going down the same path I had once taken, since she was still living with her mother. Negative energy impacts in multiple ways, with the most visible sign being to see everything and everyone else as wrong. This consumes one's own life and the possibility of a happy life.

My thoughts started to flow. From her childhood up until my marriage break-up in 2018, even if someone teased her, the harshest word I ever heard from Kumudu was 'that is not very nice'. It is evident that a parental marriage break-up affects everyone, including the grown-up children.

That innocent girl had died, and a violent woman had been born. Just a few short years ago, she would joke with me, laugh with me, tease me, bake lamington cakes for me. When asked for a second slice, she pretended not to give it to me because of my diabetes but then happily gave me another saying, 'That's all for today.' Surely, she could be reborn again back to her real nature – an innocent and compassionate woman. That was the true Kumudu.

The simplest thing to do is to think positively. See the positive side of everything. In this world, two people can see the same object differently. It is nothing to do with the object. It is how we perceive it. It is subjective – the way the perceiver's mind sees it, not the object itself. It was not Kumudu talking, it was the ego. The ego said, 'Don't meet people who you have not had anything to do with.' What would this 'ego' do if Kumudu met a childhood school friend who she hadn't seen for the last 20 years? Simply ignore the friends she once loved? I felt very sorry for her; she was carrying unnecessary weight on her shoulders, but she would recover as she is a strong and brave, hard-working girl. No one could help except herself and her own understanding. She needed time.

It is not difficult to see how the ego works; it's very cunning, making it difficult even to identify. Just taking one or two quiet minutes and inquiring 'Who am I?' – 'Is it my body refusing to meet people I have not seen for 20 years? My hands, limbs and head, or is it some other part saying, no, don't go.' It is certainly not the body. Is it our thoughts? Yes, may be. Are we, our thoughts? Thought come and go, they rarely stay with us for long. Some say we have up to 60,000 thoughts coming and going each day. Then which one of those thoughts are we? But if we are not our thoughts, then who are we?

My sister is not toxic – there are many lessons to be learned from her life experience. I know Australians are known for their love of the outdoors, their café culture, the easy-going and friendly attitude. Australians place high value on friendships and are relaxed and casual. It is about appreciating the good things in life that are right in front of you. You would be Australian if you could take a laid-back attitude to your father, who gave everything in life to make a comfortable western-style middle-class life, hiding all the pain he had gone through silently. It would be very different if Kumudu could say, 'Oh, we have not seen our aunt for 20 years, but she used to send me dresses from Sri Lanka and children's books for us to learn from.' That was the way an Australian would react, keeping the family bond and enjoying life together.

I grew up with seven siblings in extreme poverty, but nestled within was an enormous love for our kind mother, who was like an enlightened being – never angry, never speaking loudly, never gossiping, never complaining, never eating before her children finished, never blaming anyone including my father who sold everything to support his drinking habit. She never uttered a single word about what she had lost – the coconut lands and paddy fields she once owned which were grabbed by her eldest brother before she even married my father. They both hailed from well-to-do families in our ancestral villages of Kannehepola and Kanumale near Kurunegala in Sri Lanka. How could the granddaughter of such a woman become so wild?

The four youngest siblings in our family – my elder brother (*Aiya*) Navé, myself, our immediate younger sister Seela and the youngest Kumari – were always together playing in the garden near the house or working in the paddy fields or home garden. I remember at a tender age, one of the common games we played was selling goods in a boutique shop. Usually, I was the shop owner. I opened the shop under the mango tree in front of the house and made a balance using coconut shells to weigh goods. Vegetables (grasses and other wild leaves), sugar and flour (sand), rice (gravel from the pit), and dried fish (pieces of timber) were for sale. My sisters came with their bags made of reeds grown in the paddy fields and 'money' (pieces of broken ceramic plates and broken clay pots). Sometimes, children from the neighbourhood also joined us as it was all great fun. Even though we were poor, we played and laughed together.

There were plenty of seasonal wild fruits available: *Eraminiya* (jackal jujube), a climbing thorny shrub grown by the roadside with dark-black fruits; *pada* (bush passionfruit known as *pada wel*); *weera* or *Drypetes sepiaria*, a species of small tree with fruit that turned from green to bright red when ripened which we found along the road or in abandoned chenas behind the house; and *ma-dan* (the Java plum tree or South Indian plum tree) which had black coloured fruits when ripened. Whenever we could get our hands on these fruits, we always shared them. We had another friend, Bula, our pet dog, to play with. After the rice harvest, we all walked throughout the fields, bay by bay, collecting abandoned and dropped rice stalks. We brought home bundles of them, and thrashed and bagged the rice. When we had collected enough, usually a few measures, we sold it to the boutique shop and saved the money in our clay-tills. This was our well-earned treasure. On some days, we would buy sugar buns and enjoy them immensely.

As we grew up, we helped the family as much as we could, in the garden and paddy fields, contributing small ways to whatever work was available. Our sisters were a big help to our mother, and they went along with her and the other village women to pick eggplants in abandoned chenas or bring home firewood for cooking. Firewood was collected and made into small bundles using *kiri wel* (black creeper) which they carried home on their heads. Thus was our childhood. We shared sorrow and happiness; we shared work at home, in the gardens or paddy fields; we shared whatever we had to eat and more than that we did our studies and homework together. It was the same blood running through our veins. We were not unique individuals; there was no independent existence for anything or anyone.

As I grew older, I won a government scholarship and went to high schools in towns and lived in school hostels. During school holiday I came home and shared lots of stories about life in the hostel, sports and school facilities; and my sisters would fill me in on life at the village school and about their teachers, neighbours and friends. From high school, I entered the university and graduated as a civil engineer. Following me, Kumari continued to study at the village school and entered the university also, doing a Bachelor of Arts degree specialising in economics. Together we planned family economics, the marriages of our sisters, Seela and Punchi *Akka* and our only brother, the education of our nephews and nieces, and more importantly, investing for the future and going back and settling in our ancestral village once again.

Being a fine organiser, Kumari coorrdinated all the weddings, including mine in 1983. When I immigrated to Australia in 1986, her own wedding was delayed as I was financially in a poor situation. After further studies, I accepted an excellent position in the water industry in Oman, which came with a healthy salary and benefit package. Before moving, I acquired Australian citizenship and managed to retain all of our family members' Sri Lankan citizenship, making us dual citizens.

When I became financially sound, Kumari's youthful years had passed, and she had never married. In 1999, a rumour spread across the siblings that there was a conflict between my elder sister Sudu *Akka* and Kumari *Nangi* with differing views expressed by family members. This resulted in most family members distancing themselves from Kumari. At the beginning of the year 2000, misfortune fell on her again as the family she stayed with in Colombo, Daya *Aiya* and Chitra *Akka,* immigrated to Australia. Kumari went into a rented annex with furniture given to her by Daya *Aiya* and Chitra *Akka*.

This difficult period was compounded when Kumari had a road accident and broke her leg, and was unable to work. During this period, two nieces came to help her. When she recovered, she decided to build her own house. She bought a land parcel from a sub-division of a rubber plantation in Malabe using her savings. Her friends, Thamara and Wasantha helped prepare house plans and agreed to provide supervision. However, there was no money to build the house. She obtained a contract to supply short eats for functions and meetings at work places and this helped to raise additional income. After her office work, she would prepare ingredients, get to bed late at night and wake early to prepare food for selling. With these earnings and by pawning her jewellery, she started to build one bedroom of the house and moved in. She had to pawn her jewellery a number of times to complete the house.

As Kumari explained: 'It was really a difficult time … and I had no money. Once I went to buy door locks and hinges for the house, and I had to walk to the central bus stand from the shop – about 5 km. My hands were cracking due to the weight of the brass hinges and locks, my legs were in pain and thought I might collapse on the road. All this suffering was because I did not have 30 rupees to hire a three wheeler.'

This story brought tears to my eyes, as by that time I was earning well in Oman, taking the family on overeas holidays – and here was my own little sister suffering. When I heard the story of what had happened from Kumari in 2019, I determined I would not listen to any rumours again no matter who said what. I said to myself: 'I will not become angry or hate my remaining siblings and any decendants of them. I will help them in whatever way I can.'

After her retirement from government service and working as a consultant, Kumari and a nephew Amila started a photo editing company providing services to the real estate industry overseas. In the beginning, she again pawned her jewellery and with the money, bought computers. Her house was used as the office. Because of their high-quality work re-touching and processing digital images and excellent, prompt client service, Elegant Media Solution (EMS) became the leader in digitally enhanced media solutions for the real estate industry overseas. With this success in business, Kumari became humbler and helped her brother and sisters, nephews and nieces and, after

Sudu *Akka's* death, became the matriarch of the family. Kumari had brought Sudu *Akka* to her house in Colombo and given her a very comfortable life, looking after her like a mother. One of Kumari's hobbies was travelling, and so far, she had travelled widely. After my wife ended our 35 years of marriage at the end of 2018, and on hearing of my depression and suicide attempt in January 2019 from Chitra *Akka*, Kumari cried and came to see me in June 2019. During every disaster that I faced, she was with me sharing the grief.

Yet I was unable to help her during the most difficult time in her life.

The journey I went through was not easy, but the collective support of my siblings and their love made me get into a successful career. Flying over 8000 km from Sri Lanka, Kumari came to see me in February and left in March. On hearing of her visit, one of my nieces who lives in the US and was at the time touring with her husband in New Zealand also came to Adelaide saying 'we haven't seen our uncle for 22 years'. Kumudu apparently lives with her mother within 3 km from where I live in the retirement village but has been unable to make a single visit to see me, even when I was sick on several occasions. How strange – Kumudu avoided meeting her aunt and cousin simply because they had not seen her for 20 years. The niece stayed with me one week and went back to the US on the day my sister went back to Sri Lanka. That was the family bond, the Australian and Sri Lankan way. The lesson I learnt in my own experience is:

'The stronger the family bond, the more successful the family'.

Keeping rigid boundaries in life leads to easy collapse. Anything that is rigid will crack – such is life. It is said it is better to be like water – to let life flow freely like a river, not holding to anything. The moment you hold on to something, you are caught.

There is no shame in being a child of Sri Lankan parents. I have taught my children to have pride for the motherland. Sri Lanka is a beautiful island with a long history of civilisation, and I took them to almost all the culturally significant and scenic places in the country. We visited relatives every year when we were in Oman. However, one can understand the empty spot inside and the feeling of a lack of close connection to one's roots. This is not unique to my children; when I have asked friends, some of them also felt that way. As I talked with fourth- and fifth-generation Australian colleagues and friends, I understood it to be more to do with class status and identity crisis than cultural status. This is more common among children of immigrants from developing countries. Some children want to become 'Aussies' more quickly, finding short cuts by drinking beer and using slang and swearing. This is 'bogan' and not really Australian, and a very common second-generation problem, they tell me. They also say: 'Ignoring your roots is not helpful to become Australian; look at us – we come from different backgrounds, different cultures, and some of us have convict ancestors, but we do not forcefully forget our roots. This country values diversity.'

My friend, Peter, said to me: 'My grandparents came here from Greece with only 2 pounds in their pocket. My grandfather worked as a labourer in the building industry and now he owns a construction company and number of apartment buildings. After becoming a millionaire, he has never forgotten his roots; he has helped all his relatives and friends back in Greece and built a school and a hospital in his village.'

Peter continued: 'You will find other similar stories in other communities as well, and I think your children are going through a difficult period, just as you have gone through after your wife divorced you.'

Time and again we hear news from Sri Lanka about some of the elite members of society now living in cities, who were in fact originally from poor families in rural villages. They do not like to visit their village, family or even visit parents or welcome them to their houses. They have a double life failing to understand and accept the simple fact in life of 'who we are', creating unnecessary stress upon themselves.

Kumari, being a single woman and having no children of her own, treats all the nieces and nephews as her children. Before coming to see me in Adelaide, she bought some dresses for Tirath's two daughters and told me about it and asked me if there was anything I needed. I sent a text message to Tirath saying the children's great aunt was coming and she would bring some beautiful dresses for the girls.

The immediate, sharp reply from Tirath was: 'Please ask her not to bring anything for my daughters; we have nothing to do with her.'

I conveyed this to her and found she was deeply hurt by it. This was the story behind the lunch with Kumudu. She asked me to have lunch with her without bringing Kumari with me. How on earth one could I do that? What about my sister's feeling if I went to have lunch with my daughter and left her behind? Kumari even told me it was okay if I went without her, that she would stay behind in the unit. But I thought, what kind of human could do that? To ask me to come without her? Surely, she could just postpone until Kumari left?

My short reply to Kumudu was: 'If you want to see your father, you know where I live; come and visit me here, not in any coffee shop, now or in future'.

This was the message that caused her such pain and anger and for which she asked me to apologise.

I accept the fact that children being upset or angry about something does not mean they do not love their father. You can still admire what he has done for you and appreciate how much he loves you. It is not a blackmail attempt; you can choose what you want. It is common in our Asian culture that we do not express negative feelings such as anger and disappointment towards adults. It is considered a sign of disrespect. I also know some mothers influence their children to avoid the father's relatives and remove them from any association. That is why there is a saying that 'bad relatives are always on the father's side'.

Poem to a lovely daughter

You painted my nails, and applied lipstick,
tied my hair in a ponytail and laughed and laughed.
The tiny finger once used to tickle,
do not point it towards your father with anger.
Be My Daughter, once more.

Don't be a broom for someone,
and let them wash their dirty linen.
Realise who you are by asking 'Who Am I?'
Come back to your real nature, compassion, and kindness.
Be My Daughter, once more.

It is not about the weighing of sister against daughter,
it is love against hate.
Arrogance and pride do not belong to you.
Come back again with your innocent smile, and
Be My Daughter, once more.

You are the daughter, but I called you, My Mother.
You were my pride, the crown on my head.
You were born with a smile and kept you happy all the time.
Before I take my last breath,
Be My Daughter, once more.

The Deeds

A short story

Nara Somaratne

A low painful moaning sound could be heard from Bandi's room. She'd been laid up in bed, sick for the last three days, and unable to eat. People said that the third day was the worst. The woman who attended her during the night was her neighbour, Emelia, a single woman whose family had been helpers for Bandi's family for several generations. In fact, Emelia lived in a house given to her family by Bandi's family. For breakfast Emelia prepared rice, *kiri hodi* (creamy coconut milk curry) and coconut *sambal* (a kind of coconut relish). Bandi sat up in bed and attempted to eat a few mouthfuls, then fell back on the bed. She had a fever, headache and general aches and pains that meant she was weak and couldn't keep her head up. As Emelia rushed out the door, she said she would return to prepare lunch for Bandi.

On the way home, Emelia met Appu, an old village farmer, on the bund between rice bays. Appu asked how Bandi was, and Emelia said, 'Not good. Her temperature is still high, and she is unable to get out of bed.'

'There will be another funeral in the village shortly,' said Appu.

'Don't say that about the little lady; she's not dead yet!' Emelia responded, tersely.

'Hmmm, everyone in the village says that,' said Appu.

Emelia ignored him and hurried back to her home.

Bandi had been born in 1920 in Kanumale, about five miles from Kurunegala, a town in the northwestern province of Ceylon. For generations, Bandi's family had lived in this village and the adjacent one, Kadurugahamadiththa. She lost her mother in 1930 when she was ten years old due to widespread epidemic – either malaria or what the villagers called three-day fever (Spanish flu) – which had peaked in 1918–19 in Ceylon when the country was under the British rule. It was not known exactly which disease it was, as both malaria and three-day fever had similar symptoms. Remnants of three-day fever still existed in 1936, and the general belief held by the villagers was that even though it was less potent, people could still die of it.

Bandi was the youngest of six siblings. As the epidemic spread, at its peak in every village two or three funerals were held almost every second week. Like most other villagers, Bandi's father had been a typical owner-cultivator farmer who had considerable land and rice fields to distribute among his children. He made the wise decision to distribute his land among his children by transferring deeds well before his death in 1931, when Bandi was 11.

The house that Bandi lived in with her immediate elder brother Awsada and her domestic helper Emelia was her parents' family home. Bandi was given the home with two acres of land. Her eldest brother Kiri lived across the other side of the paddy fields close to the Maguru Oya – a tributary of the Deduru Oya – with his wife Tikiri and two daughters, Bandari and Bisa. The second child of Bandi's parents was Menike, the eldest daughter, who lived next door to Kiri with her family. Almost every day Menike visited Bandi, with her two children Kuma and Banda, to see how she was getting on. Sometimes she stayed overnight attending to Bandi's needs.

Like any other typical village in the area, lower valleys were for paddy fields where rice was cultivated during monsoon season. At other times vegetables, cowpea, millet or mung beans (green grams) were grown there. People in the villages believed that changing seasonal crops enriched soil fertility which was good for the next season of rice crops. Bandi's house was located on slightly higher ground. It was a cadjan thatched large house, with three bedrooms, a large kitchen and sitting room, and veranda. The plastered walls were painted white. A hall connected the veranda and the traditional paddy barn (*bissa*) at the very end. This was typical of the well-to-do villager, to store paddy after the harvesting. In this area, there was a day-bed, farming equipment and a clothesline used during rainy season. Most of the time Awsada slept there, as it was cooler than inside the house during the night.

The garden was just over two acres, typical of home gardens in the area. Curry plants, ginger, *rampe* (pandan), lemon grass and cardamon bushes were grown close to the kitchen. Beyond this, there were two jackfruit trees that gave year-round food.

Initially young jackfruit was cooked as a vegetable in coconut milk, and this was one of Bandi's favourite dishes. When the jackfruit become more mature, it was used for *mallum,* a salad cooked with freshly grated coconut. As the jackfruit further matured, the finger-like projection of flesh attached to the skin were removed and eaten just boiled, or cooked into a delicious creamy curry with coconut milk. A completely ripe jackfruit was eaten as fruits and seeds either boiled or eaten as a curry.

Bandi looked after her home garden well, just like her mother did. She grew seasonal vegetables in open spaces in the garden as her mother had done. Almost everything in the garden could be used in cooking. All essential vegetables, be they root vegetables or leaves for *mallum,* were available in the garden. The home garden consisted of annual, biennial and perennial crops. The coconut trees were further away from the house and the bread fruit tree was in the front yard of the house. The water well was located at the lowest part of the land, close to the paddy fields. Next to Bandi's land was the paddy field given to her by her parents. There was no land access connecting the two sides of the family lands, but the bund separating the rice bays was large enough to take even a bullock cart, so it was used as the connecting road. The cattle and buffalo owned by Bandi's father had been given to his sons, and the eldest, Kiri, got most of them.

Bandi was like her mother, soft spoken and charming, a fair young lady of sixteen in 1936. She and her sisters wore traditional half sarees with puff-sleeved white jackets, since wearing dresses was considered indecent by the villagers. She wore the two silver bangles her mother had given her on her deathbed six years before – the same bed where Bandi slept now.

On hearing that Bandi was sick and taking a turn for the worse, Kiri came to see her. He had a long envelope in his hand. Kiri was tall and well-built just like his father. He had a large moustache and deep commanding voice. He was wearing a *sarong* and a shirt, a folded white towel on his shoulder, as if he was going to Kurunegala town. On seeing his arrival, Awsada who was sitting on a bench in the front yard under the bread-fruit tree got up in respect. Kiri's wife, Tikiri came shortly afterwards. Kiri asked Bandi how she was, and Bandi replied, 'Still the same.'

Kiri said that he was going to town to get medicine for her fever. In order to get the medicine, he asked her to sign the papers he brought. Unable to read or write, Bandi placed a thumb, painted with ink brought by Kiri, on the papers. In Ceylon in the 1930s, rural women were not encouraged to go to school. Instead, they learned housekeeping, sewing, cooking and weaving from their mothers and the other elderly women. Bandi was delighted, since her father had died five years ago, to have her elder brother looking after her. She was so happy she fell back into the bed again and went to sleep until Emelia woke her up after mid-day for lunch.

She told Emelia that Kiri had gone to town to get medicine for her and that she had signed the papers for this. Emelia was surprised but didn't say anything and gave Bandi her lunch. It was delicious, rice with drum-stick curry cooked with coconut milk, fried salted dry fish, one of the delicacies Bandi loved, and left-over sambal from breakfast. Later in the day, Kiri brought the medicine – a mixture in a bottle – and asked Bandi to take a spoonful three times a day, then he left.

On the fourth day, Bandi could walk around the house. Her eldest sister Menike came with Dasa – Tikiri's younger brother – to see her. When asked, Bandi said that she was much better now and told them that Kiri had brought some medicine from Kurunegala and she had signed the papers.

'You signed the papers? What papers?' both Menike and Dasa asked simultaneously, with surprise.

At that moment, Tikiri also came in to see Bandi and talk shifted to the building of Dasa's new house. Dasa and Tikiri hailed from the village of Kannehepola along the main road to Kurunegala, about a mile away from Bandi's house. Tikiri was the fourth child of Ukku, and Dasa was the fifth child. The youngest of their family was Punchi who lived with his parents. Ukku had a large, tiled house in the village. It was said the family's ancestors were Brahmin, who had come from India during the period of the Kurunegala kingdom. As such, Ukku and his brothers owned a large amount of coconut lands and paddy fields in the area. It was also said that about one-third of the village land once belonged to Ukku's family. Thus, they were considered rich locally.

Dasa had completed grade 8 at school and opted to look after his lands and paddy fields instead of doing teaching or clerical work. In the 1930s passing grade 8 was sufficient to obtain a government job. He was just 22 years old but very good at farming. Dasa call Tikiri '*Heen Akka*', meaning youngest of the elder sisters. He helped Tikiri to prepare paddy fields using plough and oxen, and levelling it by using oxen and a tool known as *poruwa* (harrow).

In 1938, Dasa and Bandi married and moved to Dasa's own house in Kannehepola, not far from his parents and younger brother's house. Bandi was not a stranger to Dasa's family.

Typically, as a family grew and the older children got married, each would be given a block of land to build a house. Usually, it was the sons who lived close to the parents after they married and brought their wives, usually from the same village or one nearby, with them. The sons would continue to help the parents till the land or prepare the paddy fields. A year later, Awsada also married his uncle's daughter in a *Binna* marriage – a marriage in which the husband joins the wife's family, where the wife inherits her family property in equal or more portion. The husband does not inherit his wife's estate which transfers to their children on her death.

After both Bandi and Awsada left the house, it was re-occupied by Kiri's family, who then lived in both houses.

In 1939 Bandi gave birth to a girl named Sitta, and began thinking of going back to her house in Kanumale. Life was much easier for her there because everything was familiar – the house and the garden, the neighbours, her brother and sister, and most importantly Emelia for help at home. After discussing it with Dasa, they agreed to live in both houses and decided to tell Kiri. The next day, carrying her daughter, Bandi went to meet Kiri at her house. First, she stopped at Menike's house to feed the little girl and together they went to see Kiri.

Kiri was sitting in the veranda chewing betelnut, and after paying her respects, Bandi started to talk.

'*Loku Aiya* (elder brother), I thought of coming back here, it is much easier for me,' she said.

'I know it's easier, but this is our house now,' Kiri replied.

Both Bandi and Menike were surprised.

'But *Appachchi* (father) gave it to me!' said Bandi.

At this, Kiri got angry, and his wife Tikiri also came in upon hearing what was going on.

'You signed the papers to transfer it to me as a gift, and now it is mine,' Kiri said loudly. 'Now I don't want to hear any more about it.'

Kiri's hidden intention was to give the house to his elder daughter Bandari when she became the right age for marriage, if she would enter a *Binna* marriage.

'You heartless scoundrel!' shouted Menike angrily. 'You took her signature when she was sick – for *this* dirty work and not to get medicine. I had my doubts at the time but never thought you would do anything of this kind. I will never talk to you again, you rascal!'

With that, she took Bandi's hand and went to her house across the other side of the paddy fields. True to her word, Menike did not talk to Kiri at all after that.

Bandi could not believe it. Kiri had in fact asked her to sign a transfer of deeds three years ago; nothing to do with medicine. It was all a big lie to get his hands on the house and land before her expected death. He had gone to Kurunegala to meet the lawyer and, on his way back, bought some common liquid medicine from a dispensary. That was it. Tears were pouring from Bandi's eyes.

'The house and land were given to me by my father,' Bandi cried to Menike. 'I thought my elder brother was like my father;

I had such respect for him. It is not just the loss of a house and land, but mistrust for my brother as well causing this pain. How can I trust anyone ever again?'

Chocking on her tears, she continued, 'All I have now are these two silver bangles from my mother.'

Menike couldn't bear it, and also began crying. Her children were at home and they witnessed the event and remembered it years down the track.

In the afternoon, Bandi walked home carrying her daughter, tears still flowing. Dasa was angry when he heard what had happened but was unable to say anything as his own sister was married to Kiri.

Among Ukku's sons, Dasa and Punchi were the only ones who never consumed alcohol, either toddy or arrack or any other intoxicant. But in the mid-1940s Dasa started to drink, initially with his elder brothers, Anada and Gunarath, and later with friends. This habit gradually expanded to the use of opium and Dasa soon became a habitual user. Opium was widely available as it was a prescribed medicine by both western and Ayurvedic practitioners. Hence there were opium shops in the towns where one could purchase it, and back then, there was minimal restriction on the sale or use of opium.

This habit resulted in Dasa spending a lot of money and needing to find more frequently. Sales of coconut and the harvest from the paddy fields were not enough for Dasa to support both his expanding family and his alcohol and opium use. He started to lease his lands to his brothers who advised him not to give family lands to outsiders; and they promised to give the lands back to Dasa's children when they were grown up. This was a good deal, Dasa thought. Finally, all that remained by 1950 was the three acres of land where his house was built, his paddy field and a two-and-a-half acre land parcel.

By this time, new settlers were being selected for the newly constructed irrigation scheme in Huruluwewa. Land and house packages were given to landless families in highly populated areas. Dasa thought starting a new life in Huruluwewa where there were no tavern or opium shops would be a good plan for the future. He applied and was selected, and the family moved to Huruluwewa in 1953. But he couldn't bear being without opium, so he frequently returned to his ancestral village to work and find money by selling or leasing his remaining lands. In 1960, only the last of his lands remained: the house and land where his family had lived. He told Punchi he was thinking of selling it and Punchi said the same old story:

'Don't sell it to outsiders. Give me the lease and once your children are grown up, I will distribute it among them.'

So the lease went to Punchi, who by this time was a rich person in the village with coconut oil and fibre extracting mills. He had modified his parents' house into a large bungalow. Dasa's eldest daughter, Sitta, did not move to Huruluwewa with the rest of the family, but stayed in the house with Punchi until her marriage. The years 1960 and 1962 had been drought years in Huruluwewa area, and most of the time Dasa lived and worked in his village staying at Anada's son Jaya's house. He would send some money to Bandi, but most of his earnings were spent on opium.

In 1961, Dasa died due to hydrophobia (rabies). The funeral was held at Punchi's house and Dasa was buried on his former land. In 1962, Kiri also died of an ongoing medical condition and Bandi alone came from Huruluwewa to attend the funeral. Bandi, who attended Dasa's funeral with her children, returned to Huruluwewa with a tremendous burden on her shoulders. She had no money and now there was no male adult in the family. Only through courage, hard work, tremendous love and the collective support of family members did they manage to overcome hardships and poverty. The youngest son of Bandi, Senevi, graduated as a civil engineer and youngest daughter, Kumari, graduated with a Bachelor of Arts in economics. They finally purchased a house close to Kurunegala and settled there. Bandi was very happy in her new place, and occasionally visited her ancestral villages.

One day in 1981 Kumari heard someone knocking at the front door. An old man was there on the doorstep asking whether her mother was at home. Kumari went into the kitchen area and told her mother that an old man was asking for her. They both went to see who it was. Kumari opened the door and let the man enter the house.

'*Punchi Aiya!*' (youngest of elder bothers), Bandi exclaimed and prostrated herself before him.

The man cried. It was Awsada.

He expressed his sorrow that they had ignored Bandi for such a long time – nearly 30 years, and Bandi reassured him it was all okay now. Bandi arranged the table for morning tea. Awsada then told her he needed an operation on his eyes and he didn't have any money; there was no one to help him. But Bandi was happy to help him – after all, he was her *Punchi Aiya*. That was Bandi – such a kind and generous soul with no bitterness in her heart, despite what had happened.

Time went on at its own pace and Bandi died in 1991. Her youngest son, Senevi, immigrated to Australia and now lives there permanently. Senevi had kept some notes on the family history and details of the lands once owned by his parents, some of which he was told by his eldest sister Sitta, and he thought of writing a book about it. But to complete such an undertaking, Senevi needed some more details about both his paternal and maternal ancestry. He thought of going to Sri Lanka and visiting relatives, but before that he asked his sister Kumari to visit and get as much information as possible.

First Kumari went to see Pema, Kiri's granddaughter, who was now retired and living in the same place where Bandi had grown up. The old house had been demolished and a new house built. Pema was a single woman, living alone. Both Kumari and Pema had been friends for a long time.

Kumari told her about the purpose of the visit and explained that family history could be traced through deeds where details of land transfers were recorded. Pema was so shocked she stumbled on her words, and Kumari could barely understand what she was saying. Realising the reason for her embarrassment, Kumari said, 'If you cannot show me the deeds, can you at least give me the registration number so I can go to the land registry office and find out the ancestry?' Pema was unable to give a firm reply to this request either.

It was a similar response from the grandchildren of Dasa's elder brother, Gunarath, when Senevi visited in 2019. He was not shown the deeds but promised he would go to the land registry office and find out the family line. However, ever since then, any talk about family history beyond Ukku has been avoided by most family members.

It is not strange, when one generation has been greedy and cheated other family members, for their children and grandchildren to be embarrassed when confronted on the subject, as they all knew what had happened. The shame generated by one generation passes through time onto the next generation.

In 2023, Senevi met Banda, Menike's son, who told him all the land where Pema now lived was once his mother's land. Menike had told him this. Dasa's land was taken on lease by his younger brother Punchi, but later transferred to his own three daughters. Eventually they subdivided and sold, and Dasa's land was in the hands of several 'outsiders', as urbanisation had come to the village. Despite this, Dasa and Bandi's children and grandchildren had done well through hard work and pursuing education, and now their families enjoyed a comfortable middle-class life.

What Bandi had to give was not money nor land, but an enormous amount of love. That was the secret to her success: hard work and love for everybody. Nothing more.

Navigating through Loneliness and Aloneness

A short story

Nara Somaratne

It was Friday 12ᵗʰ January 2024 when I received a phone call from Jeff, a long-time friend and former colleague who lives in Mount Gambier, a regional town in South Australia.

'Hey Senevi, Jacki and I are in town today – shall we meet at the Central Market for lunch tomorrow?' said Jeff.

'Of course, I'd like to see you – it's been a while,' I said.

'Remember, five years ago we had a lunch there. Today is supposed to be your fifth death anniversary,' Jeff said, laughing at his own black humour.

He apologised for the short notice and said that some other former colleagues of ours, Tom and Kate, had returned to Adelaide for summer and would also like to join us for lunch.

'Fantastic,' I said, as I had not seen them for about four years.

Tom and Kate had been close colleagues of ours working on water projects. Apparently, Glenn, another colleague, was not in town and had sent a text message to Jeff regretting being unable to come. They had all retired and were enjoying travelling the world. Jeff and his wife had just returned from New Zealand and Tom and Kate were living in the UK, but had come back to Adelaide for a summer holiday and to spend time with their grandchildren.

The marketplace was crowded as it was the first Saturday after the Christmas and new year holidays and the shops had just re-opened. Jeff suggested we go to the Chinese restaurant across from the markets on Gouger Street so he could enjoy his favourite sweet and sour pork. But Kate had a different idea; she wanted to go to the next-door Thai restaurant where they had upstairs tables so we could talk peacefully. We all agreed conversation was important and we all liked Thai food as well, so we went with Kate's idea.

After a brief discussion about their holidays, the focus turned towards me and the remarkable recovery I had made since my depression and suicidal ideation of five years ago. Kate said she and Tom had both read the manuscript of the book I had written based on my life experiences, *A Silent Pain*, and said, 'What a journey through life you've had!' to which Tom added, 'Why didn't you divorce her years ago?'

To which I had no answer.

Five years ago we had all met here at the Central Markets to discuss my planned move to a 'home for elders' in Sri Lanka after my wife left me at the end of 2018, which led to me becoming depressed and contemplating suicide. My former colleagues had advised me to stay in Adelaide as help would always be available here, and that it would be better not to go back to Sri Lanka as life would be difficult with my ongoing medical conditions. I took their advice and ended up moving into a retirement village here in Adelaide.

'We were worried about you, particularly being a cardiac patient, facing this depression. It was about a year after your bypass surgery that she left, wasn't it?' Jeff asked.

'Yes, indeed' was my short answer.

One thing they all mentioned was that they were glad to see me smiling again. I was one of the lucky ones who had managed to turn the situation around. My cousin was not so lucky – said Kate, he had gone through a similar marriage breakup and depression, but he chose the wrong path, as some people do. He sought relief from the bottle, drinking alcohol more and more heavily, till finally he ending up losing his life.

'How are your children now?' Jeff asked.

'They are adjusting to new lives – the separation and divorce was not easy for them either,' I said.

'I noticed in your book that your children kept silent most of the time or took their mother's side when it came to an issue,' said Kate. 'It was particularly sad to notice when you were planning to go to Oman for that job with the oil company. You were not going on holiday; it was all for them.'

Tom looked at me thoughtfully and said: 'Family issues between a husband and wife always arise; sometimes Kate and I don't even talk to each other for a day. But by the following day, it's usually over. And if it was our children, they'd say, "You're wrong, Dad" or "You're wrong, Mum" straight away. That was the strange thing – I never noticed that kind of response from your children in your book.'

He paused to take a bite of the delicious Thai lunch, then asked: 'Anyway, how did all this begin? Writing a book, I mean,' Tom continued. 'We all know you've written lots of technical papers for journals and conferences, but that was all about groundwater!' he laughed.

'Well, the short story is, I was writing my family history for several years and in it I wrote about my childhood struggle with other family members. Then a thought came that I must expand it to a book.'

'Are you going to write any more books?' asked Kate.

'Yes, currently I am writing some short pieces, again turning some of my life experiences into short stories, before getting into environmental stuff. I feel like there are lots of lessons to give to society from my life experience.'

'Why don't you write about how you navigated through the depression, particularly the loneliness that led to suicidal thoughts?' Kate suggested. 'I think that would be interesting reading and a useful lesson for everybody, as we all undergo some degree of loneliness in our lives,' Kate said, before she left, and her suggestion stayed with me.

Going back to what happened five years ago was not easy. I was alone in a large house in a large garden with no one to talk to, I wasn't going out, I wasn't eating or sleeping well. It was a continual bombardment of thoughts about the family breakup. I had lived alone before, in Oman twice, over a year each time, when my wife and children were in Adelaide. The major difference was that I was socially connected to the family then. I saw them through videoconference at least four times a week, and I talked to them over the phone. And more than that, I knew they loved me and there was a purpose in my life. The rest of the time on weekends, I spent shopping, cooking, cleaning the house, washing and ironing, watching TV news and travel documentaries, and listening to music. I missed my family, but I didn't feel lonely. In fact, I was delighted when I heard the children were doing well in their studies and other activities and couldn't wait to hear from them again.

Back in November 2018, after my wife left, I was okay for the first few days, but gradually felt the need for someone around but I wasn't clear what for. I telephoned my wife, Suramya, and asked her to return, but she declined. She said she couldn't because our elder son Tirath, who she was staying with, might become angry.

My mind became pre-occupied with the happy times we had together, and within a few more days, a feeling of laziness started to appear. Cooking was the first thing to go and watching TV was the next. Sometimes I would just have the TV on to hear some 'noise' rather than watching whatever program was on. I had grown up in a large family and then had my own family, and other than Oman, I'd never lived in isolation, but this time, it was only me.

The house was so silent I sometimes I took the folding chair to the balcony and sat there for hours looking at the passing cars and occasional street walkers. I suppose it was a way of feeling connected to humanity. We had not been socially connected in Adelaide since my wife had a falling out with her brother and sister-in-law. The Sri Lankan community organised various social and religious events but Suramya's brother was an active member and always there with his family, so she did not want to go. Thus, the only people I knew were a few friends and colleagues from work. Since my youngest son, Sirimath, who had been in Adelaide for the Christmas holidays, had gone back to Melbourne where he lived and worked, the social isolation felt very strong.

On some days I went to West Beach for a walk along the promenade and spent time watching the people playing on the sand and swimming in the ocean. Other days, I went to Hackham East and Christies Beach to see places we had visited when Tirath was small such as his kindergarten and playground, to refresh my memories hoping that would help me to revive.

Nothing helped.

As every hour passed, more negative feelings arose and I found myself wondering what would happen if I got sick, and why no one loved me or offered me help of any kind. My mind was always pre-occupied with my wife, my children, my grandchildren, my job, my education and so on. The thoughts would swirl around and around in my mind. It was never ending …

Yet these were nothing but self-centred thoughts leading to fear and loneliness, as Jiddu Krishnamurthi described … but the thing is, I didn't know that then.

There were friends and colleagues at work I could have contacted, but I did not feel close enough to them to talk to them about my innermost thoughts and feelings. Then, by the middle of the second week of January 2019, I had started to feel deeply that I had no meaningful connection in the world at all.

The only thing that had given my life meaning was my family, and now they were gone. I also feared the imminent loss of my employment, since I had no savings after working over 40 years; further the condition of my health was worsening with age, adding even more fuel to the fire. All of these feelings caused tremendous mental pain and agony, day and night – I felt like I couldn't escape it. When it became utterly unbearable, a thought crossed my mind that suicide was the only solution to relieve the pain. I couldn't see or think about anything else. This was the peak of the depression, and the mental pain was increasing hour by hour exponentially. Being lonely in a strange place is understandable, but in my own home, and in the suburb and city that I lived over last 20 years … it was unfathomable.

I planned in detail how I would kill myself, and got everything ready … but then I fell asleep and accidentally missed the moment I had planned for.

Instead, that very day upon waking, I forced myself to make contact with some old friends in Brisbane. After some long discussions, I followed their advice and started to meditate to calm my mind, initially at the Sri Lankan Buddhist temple in Crafers for three days, followed by every Sunday morning at the Tibetan Buddhist centre (Buddha House) in Magill. In addition, I started listening regularly to profound philosophical talks from Buddhism on emptiness and letting go, Taoism on flow and non-dual Vedanta. I also listened intensively to Jiddu Krishnamurthi on loneliness and fear. As Krishnamurthi emphasised, love and compassion heal pain and fear, dispel darkness and neediness, and bring a new rhythm of sweetness, peace and joy to oneself.

Since that time, love and compassion have become a part of my daily habit, gradually transforming me into a person who looks at life in a different way. I deliberately look at the positive side of everything. There is nothing for us to hold on to; everything changes and is impermanent.

As life became easier, anger and loneliness started to dispel. There was no reason to become angry and I have not been angry since 2018.

Not by any means have I yet become a perfect person, but I am a more relaxed, stress-free person. A family connection to Sri Lanka has been established and I am constantly in touch with friends who live elsewhere. I have started to participate in social gatherings in the community and, more importantly, started to do an exercise program and joined a gymnasium instead of merely walking in the street.

This gradual transformation has given me a new lease on life. I have started doing all the normal chores around the house – cleaning and cooking – and more importantly I am back to eating healthy food. One of my childhood dreams was always to travel the world, which I have restarted doing and so far, I have visited many locations within Australia and several countries around the world. In my free time I have written a family history book and the fictional-style life story *A Silent Pain*; both are now completed. Writing has become another hobby, and feel I have something to give society through my written words, which gives my life a further sense of purpose. This new life is beyond mere existence, breathing, eating, sleeping and working, and it is doing everything with joy. I feel in every moment that I am living again.

As I adjust to these new circumstances, feelings of fear and loneliness may have passed, but they persist in different ways. Sometimes I feel like talking to someone or reaching out to catch up with someone for a coffee. These are feelings similar to when one feels alone in a group if you do not know anyone to talk to. When I feel this way, I sometimes walk or drive to a nearby coffee shop, or go outside and sit on the bench, or go to the gazebo and listen to the blackbirds sing or simply watch my thoughts flow. Watching your own thought flow is interesting, as there are moments experienced without any thoughts, a complete silence which brings extreme happiness. If we start to enjoy our solitude this way, we don't feel alone. Aloneness is inner aloneness; one is alone in one's own mind. It is interesting to see what happens if two alone people meet, will they still be alone? According to Krishnamurthi, aloneness remains as long as ego exists, so we must adjust to life with it.

Not understanding how the mind operates nearly took my life five years ago. Loneliness was just my mind attacking itself; it was the constant flow of self-centred negative thoughts about my wife, children or any situations that arose at the time. It was an absence of love, care and social interaction.

Not being able to understand this, I nearly lost my life.

Silly me.

Author's other published works

1. *Narayana Family – Brief History and Demography* (with Kumari Narayana)

   Distribution to Narayana family members

2. *A Silent Pain*

   Order from: https://inspiringbookshop.com

Forthcoming publication:

Howl of the Last Fox